Arthur Young and the Corgi Mystery

W0289027

Access all the accompanying digital components for this book on **allango**, the DELTA Publishing language learning platform:

Scan the QR code or go directly to **www.allango.co.uk** | Search for the title or the ISBN and click on the cover image | Access content, use now or save for later

When you see this symbol, accompanying digital content is available.

DELTA
Team
Readers

Don Haupt

Arthur Young and the Corgi Mystery

DELTA Publishing

Abbreviations

sth = something
sb = somebody

Contents

Team read

Choose one of the following characters and tick the box.
Read only your character's chapters and those chapters that *everybody* has to read.

Everybody has to read these chapters (A): Prologue, 1, 2, 3, 10, 11, 15, 16, 17

Of course …

You *can* always read the whole story and discover everything that's going on for yourself!

Read chapters for (L): 4, 7, 12

LYV SAVAGE

Choose to follow Lyv if you do not read books very often or if you feel that long texts in English are confusing. Lyv is the cop you want by your side in iffy situations. She's got some seriously good karate moves – as the butler finds out. But did the butler *really* do it? ☐

Read chapters
for (H): 5, 8,13

HIGGS DUNCAN

Higgs is good at reading the evidence, he sees the things others often overlook. If you sometimes read books or if English is not really difficult for you, follow Higgs's chapters. Will he find that one clue that solves the case?

Read chapters
for (A): 6, 9, 14

ARTHUR YOUNG

Arthur's a good cop and loves his job (and doughnuts!) but sometimes he jumps to conclusions too quickly. If you read a lot or if English is really easy for you, read Arthur's chapters. Will he follow the right leads and manage to save Skiddi in time? The Queen is counting on him …

Before you start

1. What do you know about the British Royal family? Who is in the family? What do they do? Is there a Royal family in your country?
2. Look at the picture. What can you see? Complete the mind map with words from the picture?

3. Can you add more words to the different categories?
4. Now read the story. Some of the pictures and the words in your mind map are relevant. When you have finished reading, look back at this page and circle any words or pictures that are connected to the story. How are they connected?

Arthur Young and the Corgi Mystery

AAAARRRGGGHHH!!!

Prologue

The scream – a very *royal* scream – shattered the Friday morning quiet in Buckingham Palace. It echoed down the long corridors and spilled onto the streets of the City of Westminster, stopping people in their tracks.

AAAAAAA

All

Chapter 1

It was still early when the team from Scotland Yard – the legendary Young Detective Squad – arrived at the Ambassadors' Entrance to Buckingham Palace.

The team was led by Detective Inspector Arthur Young, the youngest detective at Scotland Yard – ever.

Accompanying DI Young was Sergeant Higgs Duncan from Forensics. Brilliant, nerdy and a talented crime scene investigator, his taste in clothes was … well … *questionable*. The bolder and brighter the colours and patterns, the better. His colleagues often had to look slightly past him – or wear sunglasses.

The youngest member of the team was Sergeant Lyv Savage. Arthur was glad to have her on his team, especially in iffy situations. Lyv was trained in hand-to-hand combat, firearms and the crossbow – although he had never actually seen her last skill in action.

The three officers were met by a warden who led the way up a flight of stairs and through the magnificent State Rooms. Valuable treasures from the Royal Collection were on display. The huge rooms were richly decorated, laid with fine carpets and hung with paintings.

ambassador sb who officially represents their country in another country | **forensics** scientific techniques used to solve a crime | **crime scene** a place where a crime has been committed | **bold** *(here)* strong | **iffy** uncomfortable or difficult | **hand-to-hand combat** a type of physical fight involving more than one person | **crossbow** a weapon similar to a bow with an elastic launching device | **warden** sb who is in charge of security in a building | **magnificent** wonderful

Young looked around nervously. He always had that uncomfortable feeling of being watched by hundreds of painted eyes when he was in a gallery.

"Only fair," he thought, "people stare at them every day so why shouldn't they look back?"

Still, he quickened his steps a bit.

Once they got to the Private Apartments the group turned right and walked along the Principal Corridor. After passing several of the 775 rooms in the palace, the warden stopped at a door guarded by two police officers. This was the door to the *Corgi Room*, where the Queen's dogs have their special quarters.

The room was already swarming with police officers and palace guards. It looked like most of the other rooms in the palace except for the raised dog baskets and a row of battered silver and porcelain dishes filled with water and leftovers from breakfast along one of the walls.

Other than the dog baskets the room contained only a couple of armchairs, a plain and rather out of place looking sofa and a large mirror. On the wall opposite the door there was a fireplace.

The room's decoration on the other hand reflected the long history of the British Empire. The walls were hung with paintings from India and the Himalayas, a couple of valuable daggers and coats of arms from various monarchies and smaller kingdoms. A row of expensive-looking vases and sculptures stood on the mantelpiece. To the left of the fireplace was another door with direct access to the gardens.

to swarm to form a big group of people | **raised** elevated, above the ground | **dog basket** a bed for a dog | **battered** old and heavily used | **leftovers** food that hasn't been eaten | **fireplace** a place in the wall used to make a fire for warmth | **dagger** a weapon similar to a knife | **coat of arms** a sign to represent a family or a city | **vase** a container used to put flowers in | **mantelpiece** a shelf above a fireplace

Part of the room was separated by a heavy red curtain that hung from the ceiling. DI Young peered behind it and discovered what appeared to be a pet spa.

A golden, corgi-sized bathtub was surrounded by shelves and counters filled with various beauty products for dogs in bottles and containers. Stacks of fluffy towels in different colours and with embroidered names lay next to the bathtub.

None of the Queen's five corgis were there, but DI Young took note of the dog toys and comfortable cushions scattered across the floor.

He also observed that the heavy carpet had some visible stains. Worryingly, they did not appear to be tea or coffee stains …

***

ceiling the roof inside a room | **towel** a piece of cloth used to dry yourself or to wipe sth | **corgi** a breed of dog | **cushion** soft and similar to a pillow to sit on | **stain** a dirty mark on sth that is difficult to remove

"Good morning, sir," said a tall, skinny constable who came to meet them.

"Good morning, Speed," the inspector replied, "so, what do we have here?"

"Sir, it appears that the Queen's favourite corgi Skiddi has been kidnapped – or worse. The dog is missing and we found a bloodstained towel by the bathtub," PC Speed said, pointing to the small evidence marker placed next to a towel lying almost as carefully folded as the others beside the bathtub.

"Do we have any witnesses?" the inspector asked.

"No, unfortunately not. The corgis' butler noticed–"

The sound of snorting laughter from somewhere behind Young was quickly disguised as a cough.

Speed frowned and continued, "*Corgi butler* Sexton noticed that Skiddi was missing. He immediately informed the Queen and a number of staff started to search the palace. Her Majesty herself noticed the bloodstained towel – that's when Scotland Yard got involved."

constable police officer | **to kidnap** to keep sb captive against their will and ask for money to let them go | **to snort** to make a strange sound in your nose | **to disguise** to hide or change the appearance of sth | **to frown** to bring your eyebrows together so that there are lines on your face which show that you are upset or concentrating

"Suspects?" Lyv asked. She was always economical with words. She liked clear facts.

Speed checked his notes. "So far we have identified three members of staff who were in or near the Corgi Room this morning. There's Sexton, of course. He's waiting next door to be questioned. Then there's the cook, Madame Soufflée. She's responsible for the corgis' diet. They both live in the palace. And then there's MacAnguish, the gardener. According to Sexton he usually lets the corgis out into the gardens in the mornings. He should be somewhere outside."

suspect sb who the police think has committed a crime

"Who let the dogs out?" Arthur was so busy scribbling down notes and trying to keep up that he missed the last bit.

"Uh … the Scottish gardener, MacAnguish."

"Uhuh, … Scottish. Well … OK. Thank you Speed," Young grunted. "OK team, let's get started." And he nodded to Lyv and Speed to follow him out of the Corgi Room to question Sexton.

Higgs, left behind to begin a forensic examination of the crime scene, threw everybody else out of the room.

A Sum it up...	Think about it...
The three most important things that happened were: 1. 2. 3.	The Queen has pet corgis. Have you ever had a pet? Do you think it's OK to keep animals as pets? Why?

Chapter 2

Sexton was standing stiff as a poker next to a desk and politely refused the offer of a chair. Clearly he took his job seriously and his whole manner reflected his sense of duty and loyalty.

While Lyv and Speed made themselves comfortable on a Renaissance sofa Young began the interview.

"So, Sexton, tell us about the events this morning. What happened and when did you discover that Skiddi was missing?" the inspector inquired. He sat down on a chair and pulled out his battered notebook.

"Shocking, sir, it was quite shocking. First the incident with the trespasser and then–" the butler began.

"Wait, what?" the inspector interrupted, "Incident? Trespasser?"

"Well, sir, *the trespasser* ..." Sexton insisted, obviously expecting everybody to know about the incident. "Sir, as every morning, MacAnguish unlocked the door to the garden and let the corgis out. He is the only one with a key to the door," Sexton explained.

stiff as poker rigid, very straight | **duty** responsibility | **battered** old and heavily used | **incident** sth bad that happened | **trespasser** sb who illegally enters sb else's property

"Suddenly there was chaos. The palace guards had found somebody wandering about the gardens. This all happened while the corgis were running around and playing outside," Sexton reported.

"I see … gardener … key …," Young scribbled into his notebook.

"A traumatic experience for the poor creatures," the butler added. "Scotland Yard were called in and they escorted the trespasser off the premises."

"So, Skiddi was still around after this trespasser incident, right?"

to scribble to take quick notes | **to escort** to go somewhere with sb to make sure they leave

"Indeed, sir," Sexton confirmed.

"What happened next?"

"Well, sir, we tried to return to our normal routine. MacAnguish let the corgis back inside, Madame Soufflée prepared breakfast for our royal pets and I went about my duties."

"Umm … breakfast …," Young noted down. He suddenly felt hungry. The image of a box of chocolate doughnuts popped into his mind.

"After breakfast I came back to collect the dishes, refill fresh water and tidy the dog baskets. Usually Skiddi is busy cleaning up any leftovers. He will eat everything, even rocks and toys, and he is always hungry. Not so today, sir …," Sexton paused. "He simply was not there," the butler whispered. "I checked the corridors and the adjacent rooms and then proceeded to inform Her Majesty – I'm sure you can imagine her shock. I then enlisted some of the palace staff in the search, sir," he finished.

to confirm to say that a fact or opinion is true | **adjacent** next to or very near sth | **to enlist** to ask sb for help

"I see, …," Young grunted. He finished sketching the box of doughnuts in his notebook and then continued: "Who else has access to the Corgi Room or was near the corgis this morning?"

"I believe," Sexton began, "Jill Banister, the pet groomer, was here this morning. That is unusual because she normally comes in on Mondays to style the royal pets. She was here this morning for a few minutes at around the time the trespasser was caught. I saw her leaving shortly after with the enormous beauty bag she always carries."

"Mmm … Jill … enormous bag …," Young mumbled taking notes again. "What about this gard–?"

Suddenly the door flew open and Higgs rushed into the room. "Boss, I found some blood on the handle of the door to the gardens," he reported excitedly. "I don't know yet whose blood it is. Or if it's human or animal blood."

Young shot from his seat. The chair that had been supporting his weight gave an audible squeak of relief.

"The gardener!" he yelled. "It's got to be the gardener! He's the only one with a key to the garden door. And that has to be the only way to smuggle a dog out of the palace unnoticed."

groomer sb who takes care of keeping an animal clean | **handle** the part of a door that is used to open it or close it | **audible** that can be heard | **relief** a feeling of happiness when sth bad you thought was going to happen, doesn't happen

Speed, Lyv and Higgs stared at their DI. He had the unfortunate habit of jumping to hasty conclusions.

"It's all quite clear – find this MacCriminal and the case is solved," Young said proudly. He turned to address Speed, "Has the gardener been questioned yet?"

"No, sir. He must still be somewhere outside."

"Well, go and find him!" Young ordered. "He may try to get away with Skiddi."

The constable was prevented from leaving by Sexton repeatedly clearing his throat to get some attention.

"Sir, sir …, if I may be so bold. MacAnguish may already have left. He usually leaves before noon on Fridays to spend the weekend at his croft in Dunbar, somewhere near Cove Harbour I believe. He won't be back until late Sunday evening," the butler informed them.

"Of course, he's trying to take the dog as far away as possible," the inspector theorised. "Quick!" Young stormed towards the doors, closely followed by Speed. "Once he's left the premises, it will be easy for him to get away."

"Uh … Boss? There isn't really any clear evidence that MacAnguish is our suspect," Higgs warned.

hasty quick, and without thought | **constable** police officer | **bold** *(here)* not scared of dangerous things or situations | **croft** a small farm

Speed, I want you to ...!

But DI Young was in no doubt. He rushed out of the room shouting orders to his puzzled colleagues.

"Lyv, find out if the cook knows anything. The gardener may have had an accomplice! Higgs, go back to the Corgi Room and find me evidence! I'll arrest the gardener and rescue Skiddi."

The door slammed shut.

PC Speed was unsure what his orders were … *Best go with the inspector*, he thought and followed him out.

A Sum it up…

The three most important things that happened were:

1.

2.

3.

Think about it…

Arthur was very hungry and even sketched a box of doughnuts in his notes. What do you usually have for breakfast?

There was an order to arrest the gardener without a lot of evidence. Do you agree with the order? Why?

puzzled confused | **accomplice** sb who helps sb else commit a crime | **to arrest** to take sb to the police station to ask them questions about a crime | **to slam** to close a door fast and loudly

All

Chapter 3

Higgs sighed.

"Oh no, he's off again. I shouldn't have reported the blood right away. We don't even know yet if the dog was kidnapped or just got itself locked in a storage room."

"Mmmpf," Lyv grunted.

"Well, I'll try to find more evidence that will shed some light on things," Higgs said and left.

With everybody else gone, Lyv made her way to the palace kitchen to talk to Madame Soufflée. After flashing her ID both women sat down in a quiet corner of the kitchen.

The cook was a rather worried looking woman in her mid-50s who nervously confirmed the butler's story. She had also witnessed the trespasser incident as she happened to be outside at the time and she had joined the search team after Skiddi went missing.

"So, after preparing the dog food for breakfast, you–"

---

storage room a room where things are kept | **to shed light on a situation** to say the truth about sth | **to confirm** to tell sb that sth is true

"Dog food? *Dog food!?*" the cook interrupted, raising her voice. "Ma'am, I will have you know that I only serve the best dishes for our royal pets. There was venison, wild goose, and salmon on the menu this morning. Freshly prepared, with fresh vegetables, balanced and of excellent quality."

"Ehm … Sure," Lyv replied. Dogs' diets, even royal ones, weren't really her thing. "Anything unusual you noticed going on lately?" she asked.

"Well, the trespasser of course," the cook shifted uneasily in her chair, "but … I also think that James, that is Mr Sexton, has been behaving strangely lately. I've heard him coming and going late at night sometimes." The cook leaned forward and lowered her voice, almost whispering her last sentence. "Our rooms are on the same floor in the servants' quarters, right next to each other."

Lyv thought this was a strange thing to say.

"Thank you, Madame Soufflée, that'll be all for now."

venison meat from a deer | **salmon** a type of fish | **uneasily** in an uncomfortable and nervous way | **quarters** a place where a group of people live

The Daily SON

Queen's Corgi Kidnapped – Or Worse . . .?

■ Bizarre goings-on at Buckingham Palace

At nine o'clock this morning a team from Scotland Yard, led by DI Arthur Young, was called to investigate a crime at Buckingham Palace. The palace has been closed to the public and armed police have cordoned off a large area. There has not yet been an official statement, but according to an inside source, the Queen's favourite corgi Skiddi has been kidnapped.
It was the second time today that Scotland Yard was called to Buckingham Palace. Just half an hour earlier guards caught a trespasser wandering around the palace grounds. Police have not commented on whether the events are connected, but did confirm that the trespasser is still in custody.

■ Franiri Kahn on state visit

Prince Franiri Kahn of the former colony of Menampur is presently a guest of the Queen while on a state visit. Since gaining its independence the small monarchy in the Himalayas hasn't always been on friendly terms with the United Kingdom. During British rule many of the small kingdom's valuable treasures were brought to England. The purpose of the Prince's visit is to improve the relationship between the two nations. Kahn is also known to be a big lover of corgis. [read more]

armed carrying a weapon | **to cordon off** to close an area so that people can't access it | **to be in custody** to be kept by the police at the police station | **former** from an earlier time

SPECIAL ONLINE NEWS

Police seek help in armed robbery

At 8:15 a.m. two masked robbers assaulted and knocked out the owner of Styles&Brilliant, the exclusive jewellery salon on Warwick Row, just as he was preparing to open the store. The thieves smashed the displays and fled with the famous *Star of Canem*, an extraordinarily rare gem worth about 150k. PC Speed from Scotland Yard was on patrol and witnessed the robbers running away and immediately gave chase. However, as a passer-by reported, the robbers got away when they split up on Palace St. – one suspect heading north, the other one heading south – leaving an apparently confused Speed standing in the middle of the road. Police are appealing for any information from the public.

Music: Concert cancelled

Justin Bieber has had to cancel a concert at the last minute, leaving fans bitterly disappointed and heartbroken. [read more]

Man City do it again

With a landslide victory over Spurs, Man City has reclaimed the top spot in the league table. [read more]

to assault to violently attack sb | **display** the window in a shop where products are shown

A Sum it up...

The three most important things that happened were:

1.

2.

3.

Think about it...

Do you think that the trespasser kidnapped Skiddi the corgi?

The cook was very uneasy when questioned by the police. Do you think maybe she has something to do with the kidnapping of Skiddi the corgi? If so, how?

Chapter 4

Madame Soufflée's interview had not provided much information. Lyv was also a bit confused by the cook's remarks about the butler.

She decided to have a look around the gardens. Maybe she could help Arthur – although she was quite certain that arresting the gardener without proper evidence wasn't very useful. But once DI Young made up his mind there was no stopping him.

A couple of minutes later Lyv found herself in front of a window with a view of a car park – she must have taken a wrong turn and ended up on the wrong side of the building.

There was movement in the car park. She spotted a figure loading something into the boot of an old dark green Austin Mini: a pet carrier with a crown emblem.

The figure squeezed itself into the car, pulled out of the parking space and turned left into the London traffic. It was Sexton!

Lyv sprinted down to the car park, jumped into her own car and gave chase. The dark green Mini was easy to spot in the traffic. And Sexton was a slow driver. A very slow driver … Lyv caught up quickly.

---

to arrest when the police take sb to the police station to ask them questions about a crime | **pet carrier** a box used to carry pets | **to sprint** to run fast

It wasn't a very long ride. The Mini went down Birdcage Walk into Great George St, past Big Ben and over Westminster Bridge. After a short distance on Westminster Bridge Rd the butler turned left into Lower Marsh and stopped the car in front of a run-down building.

The sign above the door read 'Bet & Shark'.

Sexton went into the betting office. He left the pet carrier in the boot.

Lyv decided to wait in the car for the butler to return.

His behaviour was very suspicious. *What's a royal butler doing in a betting office?*

Sexton reappeared a few minutes later and drove off again – closely followed by Lyv.

This time the trip took a lot longer and led all the way to an old, run-down warehouse near Enderby Wharf. The butler parked the car, took the pet carrier out of the boot and pushed open a huge steel door.

Lyv waited a few seconds and followed him in. Inside she found a labyrinth of boxes, pallets and containers, some piled up to 30 feet high.

She crept forward each time the butler rounded a corner. After a while she could hear voices. She stopped at the corner and listened.

"This is not acceptable," she heard the butler shout.

---

betting office the place where people put money on who will win sth | **suspicious behaviour** behaviour that makes you think that sth strange is happening | **warehouse** a place where products are stored before they are distributed | **to creep forward** to move slowly and cautiously

"Take it or leave it," someone else hissed.

Lyv needed to see what was going on. She decided to climb a stack of containers, about 10 feet high, to get a better view.

From above she could see the butler having an argument with a bald, fat man sitting behind a table. The carrier bag was in front of him. Scattered on the table lay a collection of towels, cups, plates and various other everyday objects.

But no corgi!

Lyv frowned. This wasn't making much sense.

Sexton had just opened his mouth to say something when a phone pinged loudly.

Lyv groaned silently. A message. Now. *Really?*

Both men looked up and immediately located her. The bald man quickly grabbed the pet carrier and threw in as many of the objects on the table as he could.

Sexton stood there, his mouth still open.

Lyv made up her mind on the spot. She whipped out her ID and yelled: "Police, you are under arrest!"

---

to frown to move your eyebrows together so that there are lines on your face which show that you are upset or concentrating | **to arrest** when the police take sb to the police station to ask them questions about a crime

The fat man sprinted for the exit. The butler, finally with it, was hot on his heels.

Lyv did not think. She did not hesitate.

She jumped …

L Sum it up...

The three most important things that happened were:

1.

2.

3.

Think about it...

Why was Lyv suspicious of the green car?

Why do you think the butler was in the betting office?

Chapter 5

Higgs was in the Corgi Room all by himself. He preferred to be alone when he gathered evidence at a crime scene; in fact, he hated to be interrupted.

There was a knock on the door.

"… *Come in,*" Higgs grunted annoyed.

PC Speed walked cheerfully into the room carrying a couple of cases with forensic equipment.

"The inspector sent me to give you a hand and instructed me to bring you the rest of your equipment," Speed explained.

"Put it on the table there," Higgs said grinding his teeth.

Speed did as he was told and put both cases on a big folding table set up on one side of the room.

The cases contained test tubes in different sizes, a camera, a spectrophotometer, a laptop, various sharp instruments, chemicals and distilled water, a torch, pens and gloves.

---

evidence sth that shows that sth is true | **to give sb a hand** to help | **folding table** a table that you can carry and make smaller | **test tube** glass containers that are used in science

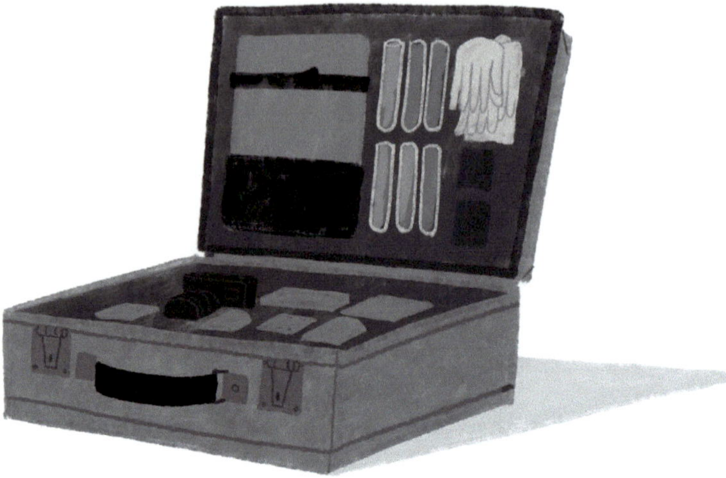

Investigating a crime in Buckingham Palace meant that you were provided with the very best forensic equipment available.

“So, what do you want me to do?” Speed asked.

“Hmm, let’s see. How about you stand over there in the corner and I’ll let you know when I need your help,” Higgs suggested and pointed towards the wall on which the two daggers were fixed.

The crime scene was probably highly contaminated with all the police and staff that had been searching the room for Skiddi.

staff people that work in a business

It still wasn't clear what crime had been committed, Higgs thought. The Queen's corgi was missing but nobody had demanded a ransom yet.

But there was blood!

On the towel.

On the door handle.

Higgs started his examination of the crime scene by standing still and scanning the room: the ceiling, the walls and especially the floor.

"Interesting," he muttered to himself.

He placed a marker next to the four dog baskets along the wall and one next to the door with the bloody handle. He grabbed his camera from the table and took some pictures. Then he took some notes and drew sketches of the room.

Next, he turned off the lights and switched on his PL500, a high intensity light source. This device can detect fingerprints, blood, body fluids and even drugs.

There seemed to be no trace of drugs.

---

ransom money that is asked for in exchange for letting sb who has been kidnapped go | **crime scene** a place where a crime has been committed | **ceiling** the roof inside a room | **device** a machine that does sth | **body fluids** liquids that come from the human body such as saliva | **trace** a very small amount of sth

But the thick carpet on the floor was almost glowing with stains of various sizes.

The PL500 also made clear that PC Speed was standing exactly in the middle of the largest illuminated stain in the room.

The constable had found the corgis' favourite spot.

Wrinkling his nose, Speed hurried to the side.

As the PL500 didn't seem to reveal any useful evidence apart from the fact that the corgis were not completely house-trained, Higgs prepared two spray bottles with Luminol. By spraying this chemical on a surface, blood will glow in the dark.

to glow to produce light continuously | **stain** a dirty mark that is difficult to remove | **house-trained** a pet that has been trained not to urinate in the house

Higgs handed one bottle to Speed and started to spray the room with the other one. Glad to finally be of help, Speed pressed and squeezed but nothing happened. The bottle seemed to be blocked.

He turned it around in his hands and squeezed the bottle even harder …

A jet of liquid shot past his head and onto the wall behind him.

And onto both of the daggers.

Another shower of drops fell onto the food bowls.

Higgs was about to yell at Speed when he suddenly stopped dead in his tracks.

On one of the porcelain dishes, still containing the breakfast leftovers, some small spots faintly started to glow. That was not all. One of the daggers also started to glow. Higgs felt excitement stir.

Bloodstains!

Ignoring Constable Speed, Higgs placed some markers, took some more pictures and started to collect the blood evidence.

From the door handle.

From the neatly folded towel.

From the dish.

From the blade. *From the blade?*

"How on earth did blood get onto the blade of a dagger which is firmly fixed to the wall?" he wondered, believing that it was Skiddi's blood.

He pulled as hard as he could but the dagger, its blade pointing to the left, wouldn't move an inch.

Puzzled, Higgs decided to run some tests: A Precipitin test, which shows whether blood is from a human or an animal. A Raman spectroscopy to estimate the bloodstain's age.

The results, however, made things even more confusing. Higgs was completely lost for an explanation.

Where did the bloodstains come from?

The results were unambiguous. None of the blood samples were animal blood. They were all of *human* origin.

So what exactly was the crime?

Fortunately, it seemed that no dog was killed in this room.

---

blade the flat part of a knife | **puzzled** confused by a situation | **to estimate** to work out, to confirm | **unambiguous** very clear

"Could somebody have tried to get the dagger off the wall to kill Skiddi and then hurt themselves in the attempt?" he thought aloud.

It didn't quite make sense but he decided to text his colleagues anyway – just in case.

> Suspect possibly has a cut on their left hand!
>
> ✓✓

Just as he pushed the send button on his mobile a piercing scream echoed through Buckingham Palace.

H Sum it up...

The three most important things that happened were:

1.

2.

3.

Think about it...

Was Higgs happy about PC Speed coming in with his equipment? Why?

Why was the crime scene probably contaminated?

Chapter 6

Arthur had sent Speed to help Higgs.

His plan was to arrest the gardener, free Skiddi and be home in time for a second breakfast.

"I have to do this bit myself," he thought. "The Queen will be very grateful. Maybe she'll even give me a knighthood."

He opened the door to the gardens, sped outside, down a flight of steps and turned left. He rushed passed a conservatory and looked around for the gardener.

There he was! Arthur spotted the Scotsman immediately – the tartan shirt was a big clue. MacAnguish was standing next to a bright yellow pickup truck. He was holding a large, suspicious sack tied with rope. He threw the sack in the bed of the pickup and climbed behind the steering wheel.

Arthur watched in disbelief. "The poor creature treated like a bag of rubbish," he thought angrily. Maybe he could catch up with the vehicle before it left the palace grounds.

The inspector started to run. After a few steps he had to slow down. Arthur had never quite kept up with Scotland Yard's fitness requirements and his love of doughnuts certainly had its drawbacks.

---

knighthood to be given the rank of knight | **conservatory** a room by the garden with glass walls and a glass roof | **tartan** a typical Scottish pattern | **drawback** disadvantage

By the time he – finally – reached Buckingham Gate, completely out of breath, the yellow pickup truck had already turned right and vanished into the heavy London traffic.

But Arthur was determined to catch the criminal. Skiddi was in that sack – he was absolutely certain of it.

He hurried back as quickly as possible to his car, jumped in and gave chase. It would be a long drive, Arthur knew. The destination was Scotland.

***

It took more than an hour to leave London on the M1 and get past Watford, and another two and a half hours to reach the A1 near Doncaster where he continued north.

There was no sign of the yellow pickup truck. However, Arthur was immensely confident. Even if the gardener took a different route, they were both heading in the same direction. Arthur was sure he would find MacAnguish's croft near Cove Harbour. So confident, that he took the time to get some doughnuts and coffee at the next petrol station.

determined when you want to do sth very much | **croft** a very small farm

When he got back to the car he put the doughnuts on the passenger seat and with the coffee cup in his hand he pulled out of the petrol station.

Suddenly, his phone made a loud noise. Taken by surprise, he let go of the cup. He shouted in pain as hot liquid spilled over his legs.

Swearing, he grabbed his mobile. A message from Higgs. Apparently the suspect had an injury on his left hand. Probably a cut.

Time passed as the inspector drove north, keeping his eyes open for a yellow pickup. So far there had been no sign of it.

Doubts began to creep in about his decision to follow MacAnguish to Scotland. Maybe it wasn't such a good idea. What if he *didn't* find him?

Also, he was out of doughnuts, so he made another stop at the service station in Berwick-upon-Tweed, about thirty miles south of Dunbar. After stocking up on doughnuts and coffee, he walked back to his car.

There it was! The bright yellow pickup truck. Pulling out of the service station.

to swear to say words that are offensive. | **to be out of sth** to need to buy more of sth because you don't have any

Arthur hastily fumbled for his car keys spilling the hot coffee over his legs. Again.

Swearing and crying with pain he jumped back into his car, keeping the gardener in his sights this time.

It was past 6 p.m. and already beginning to get dark. After about another 20 miles the pickup left the A1 and drove a couple more miles down the road before turning right onto a narrow road. A dead end.

Arthur stopped the car.

He waited about half an hour then drove slowly down the road with his lights off. The road ended just above a cliff. He parked next to the gardener's pickup, got out and walked towards the edge of the cliff.

to fumble to do sth with your hands in an awkward manner

The sea spread out quietly before him. In the moonlight he could make out a small croft down below. There was no light inside the croft. A path wound down the cliff and seemed to be the only access to the building.

“No escape,” the inspector muttered. “Gotcha!”

He stepped onto the steeply winding path. It led past the back of the croft. At that point it was almost level with the roof.

Arthur stopped to listen. Except for the faint lapping of the waves there wasn’t a sound.

Arthur eyed the roof. It was only a foot or so away. He decided to test its stability and carefully placed a foot on the tiles and pressed down. Nothing happened. The roof seemed to support his weight. A surprise attack from above would clearly be to his advantage, he thought.

Cautiously he stepped onto the roof. *Careful now…*, Arthur thought to himself.

He climbed further up the roof to get a view of the front of the croft. It was going well until …

CRASH

---

to be level to be at the same height as sb else | **faint** very quiet | **tile** a small square made of a hard material used to cover the floor or a roof

The roof did not, in fact, support his weight.

For a split second Arthur felt as though he was standing in mid-air above a gaping hole. In reality he plummeted through the roof.

"*Aarrgghhhh*!"

And then suddenly he was no longer falling … *something* had unexpectedly stopped his fall.

Arthur found himself swinging a few feet above the floor, caught up in … a fishing net, he realised, judging by the dried, crumbling starfish and some rather smelly seaweed.

At least I'm in one piece, he thought, *but eww, what a stink!*

It was dark inside the croft. Suddenly the door swung open. Arthur tried to twist round to be able to see better. In the dim light he made out a dark muscular figure in the doorframe.

A figure holding an axe in his left hand!

split second a very short moment | **to swing** to move forwards and backwards | **to crumble** to break into very small pieces | **seaweed** plants that grow in the sea

Arthur gulped. Trembling, he fumbled for his ID inside his coat pocket.

The dark figure moved forwards … *slowly*.

Arthur pressed his ID against the fishing net. "Po…Po… Police! You are under arrest!" His voice did not sound convincing.

The figure came closer. Arthur gathered his last ounce of courage and squeaked out in a high-pitched voice,

"Give up, you are surrounded by the police. You have the right to remain sil–"

The arm holding the axe rose. Arthur still couldn't see very much but he saw the blade flash in the dim light.

The hand holding the axe was bandaged …

to gulp to make a swallowing movement because of nerves or surprise | **courage** braveness | **high-pitched** higher than usual | **to be surrounded by** to have sth around around you in every direction | **right to remain silent** the legal right to not say anything when you are arrested

A Sum it up...

The three most important things that happened were:

1.

2.

3.

Think about it...

How did Arthur plan to become knighted?

What does Arthur think is inside MacAnguish's bag?

Chapter 7

The angle was correct. The distance perfect. The timing exact.

The butler's reaction – completely unexpected.

Sexton suddenly turned around and brought up his right leg. His foot slammed into Lyv's stomach. At the same time he grabbed both of her arms, sank onto the floor and rolled backwards, catapulting Lyv over his shoulder into the table and chairs behind him.

Surprised, Lyv struggled to her feet. Her whole body hurt.

She had definitely underestimated the butler.

Lyv kicked aside a chair and faced her foe.

The butler ran at her with his fists raised. Lyv blocked a left swing. But she couldn't avoid the foot that connected with her stomach. Again.

"Oof!" Lyv struggled for breath. "Where … the hell … did you … learn to fight?"

---

unexpected a surprise | **to slam** to hit hard | **to struggle** to find sth difficult to do | **to underestimate** to incorrectly guess the real value or difficulty of sth | **foe** enemy | **fist** when your fingers and in thumb are in a tight ball so that you can hit sth

She stepped to the side to avoid another swing.

"*Mortal Kombat*," came the answer, "Xbox."

Sexton was mocking her.

He raised his arm again. This time Lyv didn't duck or jump away. She moved right into her attacker and drove her elbow into his ribs.

In one smooth move she spun around and pulled him from behind. She heard his jacket rip. Sexton staggered backwards.

Lyv didn't stop.

She lunged at her opponent before he found his balance again. She pounded at his chest, spun and swept his legs from under him. Sexton landed heavily on his back.

Lyv threw herself on top of him. She grabbed his wrists and pinned him down against the cold, hard floor.

But the butler was bigger and obviously not ready to give up yet. He managed to get a hand free, slammed it into her face and pushed up.

Suddenly Lyv found herself flying backwards through the air. Again.

---

to mock to make fun of sb | **to spin** to make sth go around in circles | **to lunge** to move towards sb to attack them | **to pin sb down** to hold sb on the floor

It was the second time she crashed into the table and chairs.

She tasted blood. She felt the ringing in her ears. Her cheek ached where it had hit the edge of the table.

Lyv had had enough. Now she was really getting angry. *Right, that's IT!* she thought.

Ignoring the aches and pains, she pushed herself to her feet and, with a roar, threw herself at the butler. Spinning in the air her foot connected with her opponent's face.

Sexton dropped to the floor.

The fight was over.

***

Cuffed, bruised and beaten, Sexton was on his knees. Slowly a look of horror crept across his face when he realised what had happened.

He was under arrest.

His career was over.

He would end up in prison.

---

cheek the soft part of your face under your eyes | **cuffed** with handcuffs on | **bruise** a mark on your skin that appears on your skin as a result of a physical injury

"Where is it?" Lyv's voice broke the silence.

"Um, … where is what, ma'am?" the butler stammered.

"Where's the dog?" Lyv repeated her question.

"Wha…. you mean … Skiddi?" Sexton asked. "You think *I* kidnapped Skiddi? I did not kidnap the royal corgi, ma'am – I have no idea where he is!"

"That carrier the fat man ran away with," Lyv said, "it's Skiddi's pet carrier, right?"

"Yes, ma'am. Indeed, ma'am," he stammered, "it is Skiddi's bag. But I did not kidnap him." Sexton paused, "I thought the bag would earn me some extra money, especially if Skiddi stays missing. I wanted to sell the bag."

"Sell the bag?" Lyv asked confused.

"Yes, ma'am. Sell it. Along with the other objects from Buckingham Palace, ma'am," the butler explained, looking at the floor ashamed.

"There are collectors who are willing to pay large sums for original objects owned by Her Majesty," Sexton continued.

ashamed embarrassed by sth | willing happy to do sth

"I see," Lyv muttered. "So you stole things from the palace to sell them and use the money for your betting obsession."

"NO! That's not … I'm not … no, ma'am," Sexton stammered. "The money was meant for somebody else."

"Hmmpf!" Lyv was a bit disappointed that Sexton didn't seem to be involved in the dog's disappearance. But she wasn't taking any chances. "Well, you're still under arrest! You have the right to remain silent …"

L Sum it up...	Think about it...
The three most important things that happened were:	Why was Sexton ashamed?
1.	Why was Lyv disappointed?
2.	
3.	

to bet to put money on the result of a game | disappointed unhappy when sth you want doesn't happen

Chapter 8

Higgs and Speed stormed through the door and sprinted down the corridor towards the source of the screams.

A door to one of the guest rooms stood wide open. Both officers rushed inside.

On the floor a man, wearing a magnificent robe, lay motionless. Blood trickled from a cut across his forehead.

Leaning against the wall stood Madame Soufflée. A tray, a cup, a spoon and some sugar lay in front of her on the carpet. She had her hands tightly pressed against her cheeks.

"What happened?" Higgs asked leaning over the body on the floor.

"Is .... is he ... dead?" the cook stammered.

"No!" Higgs replied. "Just unconscious."

With help from some members of staff Higgs and Speed lifted the man onto his bed.

magnificent very beautiful | **robe** a long piece of clothing worn at home | **to stammer** to say sth with unusual pauses because you are nervous

The man stirred, slowly lifting his left hand towards the cut on his head. He opened his eyes and groaned.

The hand was bandaged.

"It's all right," Higgs soothed. "A doctor is coming. What happened?"

"I … I'm not sure," the man said. His features were Asian. "I think … I slipped … on something. I don't remember."

"The doctor will be right with you." Higgs moved away from the bed and scanned the floor. He spotted an object that looked like a squeaky dog toy. Higgs picked it up and asked the cook to follow him outside.

"What happened?" Higgs asked again.

"I don't know. I knocked on the door to serve the tea. But when there was no answer, I thought he might be asleep." Madame Soufflée explained still trembling. "I was going to leave the tray, so I let myself in. I found him lying on the floor. That's it really."

"Who is he exactly?" Higgs wanted to know.

"That's Franiri Kahn, sir, the Prince of Menampur. He's currently here on a state visit." Madame Soufflée explained.

to stir to begin to move very slowly | **to sooth** to make sb feel comfortable and calm | **to slip** to accidentally slide | **squeaky** that makes a high pitch noise | **to tremble** to lightly shake because you are afraid

"Do you recognise this?" Higgs held up the toy he had found on the floor.

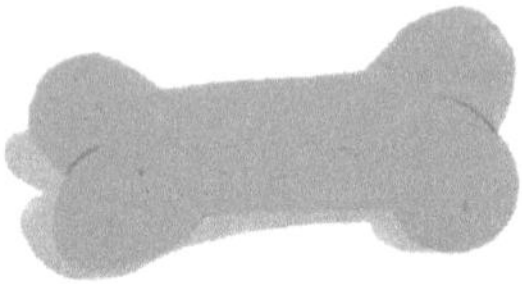

"Yes, … yes I do," the cook said, "it's Skiddi's favourite toy."

"How did it end up in the guest room?"

"I don't know, sir," the cook replied. "The prince is known for his great love of corgis. Maybe he played with the dogs," she suggested. "There's a rumour that he wanted to make an offer for one of the Queen's corgis. Of course, the Queen would never accept," she added.

***

Higgs and Speed slowly made their way back to the Corgi Room.

"Get me an appointment with Franiri Kahn, Speed. For tomorrow morning. That is, if he feels well enough again."

"Yes, sir."

"And get somebody to pick up my equipment and send the blood samples to the lab."

"Okay, sarge."

"And Speed, place a guard in front of the Corgi Room. Day and night. The other corgis might be in danger." Higgs paused, "Course, you'd have to ask for the Queen's permission first."

"Will do, sarge," Speed replied and trotted off.

Higgs looked at his notebook. He couldn't make head or tail of the evidence he had collected so far.

He had found traces of blood in four different locations in the Corgi Room.

So far, so good.

However, the blood was human, so presumably no animal had been killed – which would be good news for Skiddi.

The blood tests also suggested that the samples came from four different people.

At different times.

The methods to determine the age of bloodstains at crime scenes are not completely accurate but the results clearly showed that the blood sample from the dagger was about 8 to 10 hours old.

sarge short for Sergeant | **to trot off** to leave | **to make head or tail of sth** to try to understand a problem | **to determine** to find the facts about sth | **accurate** exact

Long before the time the corgi went missing.

The other blood samples were more or less the same age – from around the time of the corgi's disappearance.

Then there was Skiddi's toy. Finding it in the prince's room was suspicious but didn't really shed any light on the crime either.

Higgs thought it was very unlikely that the royal pet would be allowed in the guest room while a statesman was visiting. So, how *did* the dog toy get there?

Even more mysterious was the fact that Kahn had an injury on his left hand.

And to add to the mystery, there was this puzzle with the *four* dog baskets.

H Sum it up...

The three most important things that happened were:

1.

2.

3.

Think about it...

What happened to Franiri Kahn? Why was he on the floor?

Why do you think there was a dog toy inside Kahn's room?

to shed some light to explain

Chapter 9

"No … noooo … stop, please!" the inspector wailed.

"Who the hell are you? What are you doing in my croft? And why are you damaging my property?" the axe-wielding figure thundered.

"I'm DI Young," Arthur squeaked. His next words tumbled out in a rush, "I'mheretoarrestyouforthekidnappingofSkiddi,"

"Kidnapping? Skiddi? What are ye on about?"

"It's a serious crime to kidnap or kill a royal pet and I will end your mischievous criminal career!" The inspector shouted, gaining confidence.

For a moment Arthur had forgotten all about the deadly situation he was in.

Suddenly, the axe came down with force and speed.

The inspector didn't even have time to scream. All he saw was the glinting of the blade as it descended.

to wield to hold a weapon looking like you might use it | **to thunder** to say loudly | **to tumble out** to come out quickly | **mischievous** naughty or badly behaved without any intention to hurt | **to glint** to reflect the light

The blade cut through the rope and buried itself in the beam. Arthur tumbled to the ground with a thud, still caught in the net.

“I havenae done anything to Skiddi,” MacAnguish said switching the light on.

Very relieved to still be alive, Arthur managed to untangle his hands from the net and he patted his body all over just to make sure every part of it was still where it belonged. Then he got up and cleaned the dust off his clothes.

“I didn’t even know the dog was kidnapped.” the gardener continued.

“I saw you …,” Arthur began, still fumbling with the fishing net over his head. “I saw you smuggling Skiddi out of the palace.”

“Impossible!” the gardener replied.

“I saw you throwing Skiddi in the back of your pickup. In a brown sack.” Arthur claimed.

“Ye mean this sack?” the Scotsman pointed at a brown sack leaning against the wall.

“Y.. yes, that one,” Arthur replied hesitantly, “…I think.”

beam a long piece of wood | **havenae** (said with Scottish accent) have not | **hesitant** not immediately because you’re not sure

MacAnguish grabbed a large knife lying on the table.

Arthur flinched.

The gardener cut open the sack.

"*Thistles!*" Arthur cried out.

"That's right, thistles," MacAnguish confirmed. "A rare species to be exact, almost extinct."

For a moment Arthur was lost for words. Then he remembered something else.

"The suspect has an injury on his left hand – so do you!" the inspector pointed out.

"Oh, my bandage," the gardener smiled looking at his left hand. "That happened when I uprooted the thistles this morning. They're prickly little buggers."

Arthur's face fell. Everything had seemed to make sense. The evidence had clearly pointed to the gardener.

What now?

Now he was stranded in Scotland.

to flinch to make a quick sudden move because you are afraid | **thistle** a type of plant with sharp pointy bits | **species** a type animal or plant | **to uproot** to remove a plant by its root | **prickly** with lots of sharp things sticking out

A

Without a corgi.

He was tired and had no idea how to make it back to London in time for the team meeting at Scotland Yard the next morning.

He slumped to the floor again. Exhausted.

Worst of all, his colleagues would have a good laugh.

Arthur took out his mobile phone and texted Lyv and Higgs to inform them of his situation.

***

MacAnguish explained that he had secretly cultivated the thistles in the palace gardens. They were dying out in their native Scotland.

The fact that he misused his position as royal gardener was not a reason to arrest him. It was best left to the Queen to deal with.

MacAnguish, a good man at heart, bore no grudge against the inspector for his hasty accusations.

to cultivate to prepare the soil and plant sth | **grudge** bad feelings | **to accuse** to say sb has done sth wrong

He even offered Arthur a few hours of rest on his sofa before he headed back to London.

First though, Arthur had to repair the roof.

A Sum it up...

The three most important things that happened were:

1.

2.

3.

Think about it...

MacAnguish uprooted a plant with lots of prickles. Can you think three other plants that have prickles?

Why did MacAnguish cultivate thistles in the royal garden? Was it a good idea?

Chapter 10

Higgs handed Lyv a £50 note.

"I told you he'd follow him all the way to Scotland," Lyv smiled.

It was 8:40 a.m. and the three police officers were having their team meeting in the inspector's office in the Scotland Yard building.

With only a few hours sleep Arthur looked tired. He poured himself another cup of coffee (his fourth) and slumped into his chair. The coffee sloshed dangerously in the cup.

In front of him on the desk lay his *thinking hat*. Arthur had bought his deerstalker hat cheaply at a flea market near Baker Street many years ago. He liked to think it helped him sort through the facts of a case.

A new decorative addition to his office was the potted thistle next to the coffee machine.

Arthur ignored it.

note bill, paper money | **to slump** to fall onto sth | **to slosh** when a liquid moves in a rough way | **deerstalker** a type of hat similar to the one worn by Sherlock Holmes | **thistle** a type of plant with many prickles

He had left the gardener's croft shortly after midnight and driven straight back to London.

Higgs projected the information the team had so far collected during the investigation from a tablet to the whiteboard. It consisted of all the evidence found and a list of the suspects:
Sexton
MacAnguish
Madame Soufflée
Jill Banister

Higgs added the name *Franiri Kahn* to the list.

"Ok, so Sexton and MacAnguish may not be prime suspects but I wouldn't completely remove them from the list," Young began.

"Sexton has been selling royal items in order to raise money – his brother's betting habit has left him in debt to some dangerous people," Lyv explained. "He was afraid that his name would be discredited and he didn't want his brother to get hurt. Get this: Sexton used to work as a security guard before he became a …," Lyv snorted, "a corgi butler. That's where he learned how to fight. I think he reacted purely on instinct. Somebody attacked him and he defended himself."

croft a small farm | **debt** money that you owe | **to snort** to make a strange sound with your nose

She continued, "And while it was fun to arrest the butler, he has been quite helpful, so I don't think we should charge him for assaulting a police officer."

"MacAnguish was cultivating plants," Arthur said, "secretly, but not illegally."

Higgs and Lyv nodded.

"What about the prince then, Franiri Kahn?" the inspector asked.

Higgs described what had happened at the palace and how he'd found Skiddi's favourite toy in Kahn's room.

"Kahn has a suspicious injury on his left hand." he pointed out. "The palace confirmed our *audience*" he rolled his eyes "with the prince at 10 a.m."

"Lyv, you go and question Kahn," Arthur ordered.

Lyv groaned. She preferred more … *physical* tasks. This was definitely punishment.

Arthur grinned, pleased with himself.

"What about the bloodstain evidence?" Arthur looked at Higgs.

to charge to officially state sb is accused of a crime | **to cultivate** to prepare the soil and plant sth | **to grin** to smile widely

"The lab confirmed my initial analysis. All the blood is of human origin. We can probably assume that the bloodstains on the door handle belong to the gardener and got there when he let the corgis out." Higgs said.

"How the bloodstains got onto the towel and onto the food bowl, I don't know. But I assume that whoever wanted to get the dagger off the wall must have an injury on their hand," Higgs explained. "The blade of the dagger points to the left, so we're probably looking for an injured left hand," he concluded.

"Madame Soufflée's left hand's injured." Lyv remarked. "I noticed it when I questioned her."

"Interesting," Arthur said. "Higgs, question the cook again. See if you can find out a bit more about this prince too. And possibly identify other suspects that aren't on our list yet."

Higgs nodded.

DI Young scratched his head.

"We've got bloodstains, we've got suspects but we're still pretty much in the dark. We assume that we're dealing with kidnapping but there's no ransom request and no motive."

The inspector paced up and down the small office. He looked at the whiteboard again.

---

to assume to say sth is true without looking at the facts or evidence | **ransom** money that is asked for in exchange for letting sb that has been kidnapped go

"We haven't spoken to the pet groomer, Jill Banister, yet," he remarked, "I'll see if she can shed some light on the events of yesterday morning. I mean, it can't get any more confusing than it already is. Can it?"

Well …

A Sum it up...

The three most important things that happened were:

1.

2.

3.

Think about it...

Do you think this was a kidnapping? Why?

Do you think the groomer will give valuable information to solve the crime? If so what kind of information?

groomer sb who takes care of keeping an animal clean | **to shed some light** to explain

All

Chapter 11

9 a.m.

A man dressed in dark clothes climbed the steps to West End Central Police Station. He wore a long overcoat with the collar turned up. A hat partially hid his face.

Shortly after he entered the building, a police officer led the man into a room with a table and four chairs.

Five minutes later the door opened again and the officer brought a cuffed man into the room. The officer left, closing the door behind him.

The cuffed man sat down opposite the man with the hat on. They talked. A few minutes later, the man with the hat got up again and left the room.

He exited the building and walked down Savile Row.

Towards Buckingham Palace.

collar the part around the neck on a shirt or a coat | **partially** not completely | **cuffed** in handcuffs

A Sum it up...

The three most important things that happened were:

1.

2.

3.

Think about it...

The mysterious man was partially covering his face in order to not to be recognised. What would you wear if you didn't want to be recognised?

Do you think the mystery man knew the men in handcuffs?

Chapter 12

As they were both going to Buckingham Palace, Lyv gave Higgs a ride in her car.
As they were driving along Buckingham Palace Rd, Higgs suddenly saw somebody walking down the street in the opposite direction.
"Stop!" Higgs yelled.

Lyv slammed on the brakes. Tyres screeched and the traffic behind her came to a standstill. An angry chorus of hooting broke out.

"What is it?" Lyv cried.

---

brakes the mechanism in a vehicle that makes it stop | **tyres** the rubber part that covers the wheels of a car

But Higgs jumped out of the car, slammed the door and was gone.

Lyv stared after him, puzzled.

She continued the short drive to the palace, showed her ID and pulled into the car park.

Lyv couldn't believe she had to question the prince. She hated interrogations. She didn't like spending time *talking* to suspects, trying to get information out of them. She much preferred *action*. Chasing leads down. Getting her hands dirty.

Sighing, she went in. A warden led the way to the room where the interview would take place. It was empty.

Already irritated with the prince, Lyv paced up and down under a huge chandelier. To one side of the ornate fireplace stood a red and gold sofa. She flopped down on the sofa and waited.

Ten minutes later the prince entered the room together with two very large, very muscular bodyguards dressed in black suits. They fixed Lyv with a hard stare.

Lyv rose from the sofa.

"Ma'am," the prince greeted her with a slight nod.

---

to slam a door to close a door fast and hard | **interrogation** a series of questions asked to get information | **leads** clues that could be important | **to pace up and down** to walk backwards and forwards because you are nervous | **chandelier** a big decorative light | **to flop down** to sit down heavily on sth

"Your Highness," Lyv replied. Gritting her teeth, she performed the slightest of curtsies. He was, after all, a prince.

"You wished to talk to me about yesterday's attack on my life?" the prince began after they had both sat down.

"Erm, yes, sir," Lyv replied. "Kind of. Amongst other things."

She took a plastic bag from her pocket. It contained the dog toy which Higgs had found on the floor in the prince's room.

"Have you seen this before?" she asked.

"No," the prince replied.

"We think you slipped on this and fell, sir," Lyv explained. "It's Skiddi's favourite toy. That's the Queen's corgi who disappeared yesterday."

"I know Skiddi," the prince said. "I met the Queen's corgis a couple of days ago, ma'am."

"Can you explain how the toy got into your room, sir?"

"No," was the short answer.

Lyv was quite sure that she didn't like Kahn. 'Arrogant' was the word that came to her mind.

---

curtsy when a woman bends in order to show respect | to slip to accidentally slide | to come to mind to think of first

“Did you see Skiddi yesterday, sir?”

“No.”

She added ‘unhelpful’ to her list of words to describe the prince.

“When was the last time you saw Skiddi?”

“Listen, young lady,” Kahn said, suddenly annoyed. “You have no right to interrogate me about the corgi’s disappearance.”

Lyv just looked at him. Technically he was right. But she needed to find a way to get information out of him. Something wasn’t right, she could tell.

Make him angry!

“I thought you were investigating the attack on my life,” Kahn said, raising his voice.

“Well, it was the dog toy that attacked you, sir. Case solved.” Lyv was enjoying this.

Kahn suddenly jumped from his seat. Anger flashed in his eyes.

“I love corgis. I have nothing to do with the kidnapping. I wanted to make an offer for Skiddi,” he shouted.

“So I’ve heard,” Lyv replied calmly. *Coolness* was her middle name. “But we both know that the Queen would never sell one of her beloved corgis.”

The anger in his eyes became rage.

to interrogate to ask a series of questions

"The Queen will give me what I want," Kahn yelled. He slammed his fist down on the mantelpiece. An 18th century porcelain corgi crashed to the floor and shattered into pieces.

There goes £10,000.

"The times when you colonised foreign countries, invaded and oppressed them and stole whatever you liked are over!" And with that Kahn stomped out of the room dragging his two bodyguards with him.

That was weird, Lyv thought. *Were we still talking about corgis?* she wondered.

L Sum it up...	Think about it...
The three most important things that happened were:	Do you think the price the prince wanted to pay for the corgi was fair? Why?
1.	
2.	Why did Khan say "there goes 10 000 pounds"?
3.	

mantelpiece a shelf above a fireplace | **to shatter** to break into many pieces | **to oppress** to treat people in a bad and unfair way

Chapter 13

Higgs had jumped out of the car on Buckingham Palace Road, just outside the Royal Mews. He had spotted Madame Soufflée walking down the road.

Quickly, he crossed the street. The cook was about 30 steps ahead of him.

The young sergeant smiled. A boring interrogation had just turned into a more exciting surveillance operation.

Carefully he followed his suspect. Madame Soufflée didn't realise that she was being followed.

She turned left onto Bressenden Pl. Then she turned left again and walked a short distance past the buildings and shops towards Cathedral Walk. There she turned right and after another short walk she reached Cardinal Place.

"What's she doing at the shopping centre?" Higgs wondered. "I hope my first surveillance job is not watching somebody buy shoes," he muttered to himself.

Madame Soufflée glanced into a few shop windows before going into a pharmacy. She came back out a few minutes later carrying a plastic bag and started to walk back towards the palace.

surveillance when the police or an investigator carefully watch sb | **to mutter** to say sth quietly

Suddenly, a man wearing a long overcoat with the collar turned up and a hat partially hiding his face blocked her path. Madame Soufflée tried to walk around him but the man wouldn't let her pass.

Higgs watched as they argued.

Suddenly the man grabbed the cook's arm and shouted at her. With his other hand he tried to pull the cook's handbag from her shoulder.

Higgs sprang forward from his hiding place.

"Stop!" he yelled, running towards the pair. "Police!"

The man let go of the cook and swung round to face Higgs, his fists raised. The first blow caught Higgs on the nose. The sergeant's legs gave way and he dropped to the ground. Madame Soufflée screamed.

"Stop! Police!" Just as the man was about to swing his fist at Higgs a second time, PC Speed came running towards them at full speed.

The man ran off. Speed followed him.

collar the part around the neck on a shirt or a coat | **partially** not completely

But the constable was back less than a minute later and reported sheepishly that the attacker had escaped. He pulled Higgs, who had blood dripping from his nose, to his feet.

"Sir, are you OK? … Sarge?" Speed asked panting.

"Yes, … yes. Thanks Speed," Higgs replied, carefully feeling his nose. This was *not* how he had wanted his first surveillance job to end.

"I was on patrol and saw what happened," Speed explained.

The two men turned to Madame Soufflée who was still trembling. Her shopping bag lay on the ground, its contents spilling out.

"Are you OK?" Higgs asked.

"I'm OK, I think," Madame Soufflée replied, trying to sound brave.

"Why did that man attack you? Did you know him?"

"I suppose he wanted my handbag. I had just finished shopping when he blocked my path," the cook replied. "He tried to pull my bag away, but I held on to it. Then he threatened me to make me let go."

embarrassed because of doing sth silly

"So, you think it was a robbery?" Higgs asked.

"I guess so," said the cook.

"Can you describe the man?"

"I don't think I can tell you much," the cook said. "I didn't get a very good look at him. He had his hat pulled down quite far. His voice was deep and rough. And he had a bit of an accent – Cornish maybe."

Higgs wiped the blood trickling from his nose with a tissue.

"Would you like to report the crime?" Speed asked.

"I'd rather not," Madame Soufflée said, nervously but firmly. "Nothing was stolen and I'm not hurt."

"Alright," Higgs said, almost sounding relieved. His nose hurt and he'd had enough for the moment. Taking Madame Soufflée to the Yard probably wouldn't lead to much in this case – nor catch the robber.

"However, this man attacked a police officer," he said to the cook. "I'd like you to come to Scotland Yard tomorrow and help us draw a facial composite. Would you like us to accompany you back to the palace?"

tissue thin paper used to clean liquids | **firmly** in an assertive way | **facial composite** graphical representation of sb's face

"No, that's all right, I'm fine. I'm just glad that you happened to be in the area to save me."

"Erm, yes. Speed was on patrol and I was, um, shopping … for shoes," Higgs stammered, pointing at a display of women's shoes.

Madame Soufflée frowned.

Embarrassed, Higgs quickly changed the subject, "Oh, one final thing, ma'am, how did you get that injury on your left hand?" he asked.

"Oh, um …," Madame Soufflée looked slightly surprised, "I cut myself with a knife yesterday, when I was preparing breakfast for the royal pets," she explained.

Higgs was satisfied. The cook's explanation sounded believable.

Speed and Higgs helped the cook pick up her shopping. Some sun lotion, migraine tablets and two packets of laxatives …

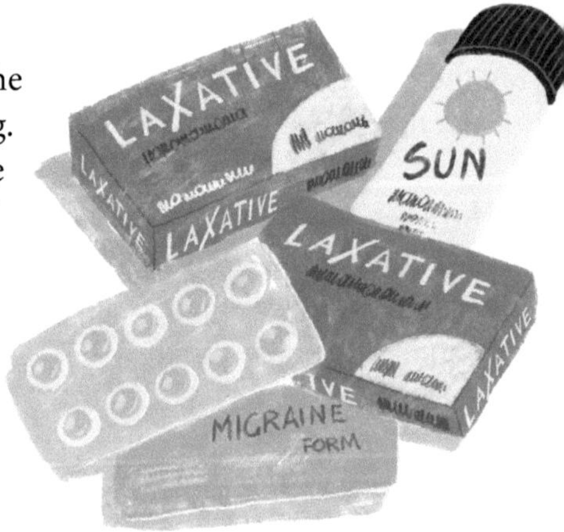

H Sum it up...

The three most important things that happened were:

1.

2.

3.

Think about it...

Why did the mystery man want to steal Madame Soufflée's bag?

How do you think Higg's first surveillance job went? Was it successful?

Chapter 14

A study of Jill Banister's driving licence details had shown that the pet groomer lived on Kenilworth Rd near Victoria Park. Arthur found a parking space a few yards down the road from her house.

Just as he got out of his car he saw the pet groomer emerge from her house. He watched her go through the garden gate and turn right to walk down the street.

Arthur decided to follow her.

Jill turned right onto Roman Rd at the next corner. Arthur hurried after her. But when he reached Roman Rd she was gone.

Confused, he turned right and slowly walked along the pavement past an estate agent and a pet store. He stopped in front of a nail salon, frowning.

"Impossible," he thought. "Where has she gone?"

He waited, continuously scanning up and down the street.

Just then Jill came out of the pet store with a large sack of dog food in her right hand. Her left hand, the inspector noticed, was bandaged.

---

groomer sb who takes care of keeping an animal clean | **estate agent** a place where they sell or rent property such as houses, offices, etc.

He didn't want to look suspicious. So he turned back to the shop window and tried to look interested in the special offer on nail extensions.

Jill walked back to her house. Arthur followed her.

"Interesting. She's got an injury on her left hand." he thought. "She bought dog food. Suspicious."

Arthur considered his next move. Should he call for backup this time or storm her house and free Skiddi?

Then he realised something. "She must be the kidnapper. She'll know that someone probably saw her at the crime scene – that she's a suspect. It would be too risky to hide the corgi at home. She'll have hidden him in a secret location. But at some point he'll need to eat. Therefore the dog food. All I need to do now is wait and follow her." Arthur was very pleased with himself.

He didn't have to wait very long. Jill left her house again and once more turned right onto Roman Rd. Arthur stayed close behind her. *Very close.* He was not going to lose her this time.

Every now and then Jill looked over her shoulder. She didn't know the man walking a few yards behind her but he definitely made her uncomfortable.

They passed Mile End Park and crossed Regent's Canal.

Suddenly Jill sprinted across the street, turned left onto Palmers Rd and disappeared.

Arthur swore. He couldn't follow her right away because of the traffic and by the time he reached Palmers Rd Jill Banister was gone – again.

He scanned the buildings. This time he didn't miss the sign that read: *Dog Daycare.*

"Very clever," he thought. "Nobody would look for Skiddi at a pet-sitter's."

No mistakes this time. He called the police station for backup. Then he waited.

After a while, Jill emerged from the building. Without a dog! But she was carrying her large beauty bag. And he could distinctly see that something inside the bag was moving.

Arthur didn't hesitate. This time, he would catch the kidnapper – and free Skiddi.

He ran towards the pet groomer, ID raised, and yelled: "Police! You are under arrest!"

At the same moment a police car shot around the corner. It came screeching to a stop in front of them. PC Speed and another police officer jumped out of the car.

---

to sprint to run quickly

Arthur pulled the bag from Jill's shoulders and opened it. Speed cuffed the terrified woman.

Inside the bag DI Young found the corgi.

Aha!

A Sum it up...

The three most important things that happened were:

1.

2.

3.

Think about it...

Why did Arthur think that leaving the dog at a pet-sitter's was very clever?

What was strange about Jill's beauty bag?

cuffed with handcuffs on

Chapter 15

It was about 2 p.m. when DI Young got back to Scotland Yard. He was obviously depressed, disappointed, his face glum and his shoulders hunched.

He had arrested and questioned Jill Banister. He had found the corgi.

Except it wasn't Skiddi.

It turned out that the pet groomer also owned a corgi – *Peach*. Jill had been at the palace the day before to get some of her equipment which she had forgotten the last time. She played with the dogs and one of the corgis had bitten her hand by accident. She had wiped the blood away with a towel which she left on the counter.

Jill did, however, admit to another crime: She had smuggled Peach into the palace, hidden in her enormous beauty bag. She wanted to breed corgis and thought that puppies fathered by a royal corgi would earn her a lot of money. Whenever she could, she tried to bring Peach and Skiddi together.

The inspector released Jill. He also released Sexton. He would write a report and let the Queen handle these internal affairs.

glum looking unhappy | **to breed** to get specific types of dog to have puppies | **to release** to set sb free

Arthur opened the door to his office. Lyv and Higgs were already there and they had brought pizza. Both grinned. Somebody had placed a bowl of peaches next to the potted thistle.

The inspector grabbed a slice of pizza and listened to the details of his colleagues' encounters with Kahn and Madame Soufflée: the attack on the cook, the items she had bought, Kahn's sudden outburst of anger and his strange remarks.

The team was frustrated. They still had no leads. No motive. No kidnapper.

And, most importantly, no Skiddi.

Arthur walked over to the whiteboard and stared at the evidence again.

Suddenly his whole manner changed. He stood up straight.

Detective Inspector Young was often quite clumsy. He jumped to conclusions quickly. And he often followed wrong leads. Arthur was the cop spilling coffee all the time. His colleagues laughed at him.

clumsy when sb has accidents because they aren't careful

But he had his moments.

And this was going to be one of them.

He sat back down on his chair (it groaned in protest) and leaned back. He put his *thinking hat* on. A light went on in Arthur's brain. A flash of genius surged through his body. The magic began.

"Hmmmm …," he muttered.

Arthur stared hard at the whiteboard. Lyv and Higgs stared impatiently at Arthur. They knew that look.

Suddenly he grabbed the tablet from his desk and scrolled through the online news.

"Bizarre goings-on … trespasser … Kahn … Man City … armed robbery … beaver …," he mumbled.

He looked back at the whiteboard. His eyes moved from suspect to suspect and from evidence to evidence, drawing invisible lines and connecting facts.

"I've got it!" he shouted.

Lyv and Higgs stared at him.

"Who's on guard duty at the Corgi Room?" Arthur asked.

flash a sudden moment

"Speed, I think," Lyv replied.

"Send him a message. Tell him to leave his post at 7 p.m. And he should do so loudly and obviously," Arthur ordered.

"What? Why?" Higgs asked confused.

"I think I know who did it – and why." Arthur said. "We could search the palace and hope to find Skiddi but then the culprit will be warned," he explained.

"I want to set a trap. We're going to catch the kidnapper tonight. Red-handed."

A Sum it up...	Think about it...
The three most important things that happened were: 1. 2. 3.	Why was Arthur very disappointed? Why did Arthur's colleagues laugh at him? Do you think it was right for them to laugh at Arthur?

culprit sb who is guilty of doing sth wrong | **trap** sth to catch sb | **red-handed** in the middle of doing sth wrong

Chapter 16

10:45 p.m.

It was dark inside the Corgi Room. The Queen's four remaining corgis slept peacefully in their baskets.

Not a sound was heard – apart from the inspector's gentle snores. Sleep had finally overwhelmed him.

Arthur, Higgs and Lyv had been hiding behind the curtains of the pet spa for almost 3 hours now.

The team had arrived at the palace shortly before 8 p.m. A warden led them through the corridors without attracting anyone's attention.

An hour earlier the corgis had had their supper and corgi butler Nestor, who had replaced Sexton, got everything ready for the night.

Speed did as he was told: at 7 p.m. he left his post.

To pass the time Higgs was playing a game of chess on his phone. Lyv was growing more bored and impatient by the minute. Neither she nor Higgs knew what or who they were waiting for. Arthur hadn't told them anything else.

Suddenly the door to the Corgi Room opened with a faint creak. Lyv peered through a tiny crack in the curtains and Higgs tucked his phone away.

At first Lyv could only make out a long shadow on the floor. As her eyes got used to the dim light she saw a figure standing in the door holding a long stick that was bent at one end.

The figure stepped through the door. Another creak as the door closed. Then a beam of light from a torch flickered over the walls, passed over the curtains (Lyv held her breath) and came to rest on the far wall.

Soundlessly the figure picked its way there, careful to avoid stepping on anything in the way.

The beam of light was fixed on a dagger on the wall. The same dagger on which Higgs had found the bloodstains.

A crowbar appeared in the beam of light. Lyv watched as the figure raised it and pulled the dagger off the wall with a short, loud crack.

The noise woke the corgis and they began grumbling and curiously sniffing about the room.

Lyv and Higgs tensed. Arthur on the other hand was still fast asleep.

faint very quiet | **dim** soft | **torch** a portable device that you can use to shine light from | **crowbar** a metal bar used to open crates or containers | **to grumble** to produce a low noise

Suddenly, the door to the Corgi Room opened a second time. The torch abruptly went out.

A second shadow appeared – smaller this time and with well-rounded hips. The figure that stepped into the room appeared to be carrying something under each arm. One of those items was wriggling around. And panting.

The corgis got even more exited. Yipping and yapping they jumped up on the second intruder wagging their tails.

“Sshhh … SSHHH!” someone tried to shush.

All this commotion was enough to finally wake Arthur from his nap. “Stop,” he yelled, suddenly wide awake. The lights in the room came on and Lyv jumped forward from behind the curtain ready to attack.

The person holding the crowbar froze. The dagger was clutched in his other hand.

“Put the weapon down, sir,” Arthur said calmly, stepping out from behind the curtain.

The man looked at the inspector arrogantly and with distaste.

“You don’t want to give Lyv a reason to arrest you, Prince Franiri,” Arthur smiled.

Lyv looked at Arthur hopefully.

to wriggle to make quick movements | **to pant** to breathe quickly after doing sth physical

A hint of uncertainty crept across Kahn's face. His eyes wandered left and right but his two big bodyguards weren't there.

"I'm not going to arrest you," the inspector continued. "It's up to Her Majesty to deal with her guest and this family treasure from Menampur which you were trying to steal."

"But I am arresting *you* for the kidnapping of Skiddi," DI Young said, addressing the other person in the room, "and for possession of stolen goods, the Star of Canem, which Skiddi swallowed in the garden – I really hope you've cleaned it – … Madame Soufflée!"

The cook stood frozen in the middle of the room. She had a dog basket clutched under her right arm. Skiddi was squeezed under her other arm.

The dog looked very happy to be back home.

A Sum it up…

The three most important things that happened were:

1.

2.

3.

Think about it…

Do you think their plan to catch the kidnapper was good? Why?

Who was the person holding the crowbar? Are they the kidnapper?

All

Chapter 17

The next day Detective Chief Inspector Norman called the team to his office. He congratulated them on their success.

“A job well done, I’d say,” he nodded, pleased.

Jill Banister lost her job. The Queen was not amused when she heard what the pet groomer was trying to do.

Corgi butler Sexton was pardoned by the Queen – but only after she gave him an impressive dressing-down and limited some of his privileges. She didn’t care much about his brother’s legs but she believed Sexton deserved a second chance. And before today he had been a good man and a model corgi butler. She had a feeling that he would prove to her that he was an even better one after this.

MacAnguish, on the other hand, got a promotion. The Queen rewarded him for trying to save an endangered plant.

Prince Franiri had already taken an early morning flight out of London. The audience with the Queen obviously did not go well. He was, however, allowed to take the dagger with him. According to Kahn it was of great value to his family as it had been used in traditional ceremonies for centuries.

---

to give sb a dressing-down to tell sb off for doing sth wrong | **to get a promotion** to be given a more important rank in a company

Madame Soufflée was in custody. She had admitted to her crimes and had handed over the valuable diamond to the authorities.

"When did you suspect the cook?" the chief asked.

"Once I found the motive, everything else fell into place, sir," DI Young explained.

"It all began with the robbery of the valuable Star of Canem. PC Speed lost the robbers when they split up on Palace St. One of the thieves headed north, towards Buckingham Palace – our trespasser."

"He somehow entered Buckingham Palace Gardens and, of course, was quickly caught by the guards," Higgs added.

valuable sth that is worth a lot | **to suspect** to think sb did sth wrong

"We're not sure yet," Arthur continued, "whether the thief panicked and threw away the diamond or whether he simply lost it during the arrest. As the corgis were playing in the gardens at that time, Skiddi found the gem and swallowed it."

"And the cook?" the chief asked.

"Well, she was basically the only witness, which she admitted herself during Lyv's questioning. She and the trespasser saw what happened with the gem."

"Then she kidnapped Skiddi!" Lyv added.

Arthur nodded. "Her plan was to keep the dog hidden in her room until the diamond reappeared *naturally*. I assume that the dog had a blockage or that Madame Soufflée got nervous and wanted to speed things up. That's why she bought the laxative when she was attacked by the second robber," Arthur concluded.

"The second robber?" The chief was confused.

to assume to think sth is true without evidence | **laxative** medicine that makes you need to use the toilet urgently and often

"Yes! There were two robbers, sir. One of them got away after the robbery. It was mentioned in the news reports. The trespasser was still in custody but the second thief must have found out what happened and started to look for Madame Soufflée. He wanted to get the diamond back but the cook wasn't very cooperative."

"But what about all the other evidence?" DCI Norman wasn't completely satisfied. "What about all the blood evidence?"

"Unfortunate coincidences, I'd say," Arthur replied. "Although it did arouse my suspicions that Kahn wanted to steal the dagger."

"More interesting was the fact that only four dog baskets were in the room," Arthur noted.

coincidence when two or more things happen in a way that is unlikely or surprising

"A clue that whoever kidnapped Skiddi didn't mean any harm. It also suggested that Skiddi was still in the palace. It would not have been possible to take a dog *and* a large dog basket without someone noticing. So it was most likely that one of the staff living at the palace was the kidnapper."

"And remember the dog toy in Kahn's room?" Higgs took up the story. "We believe that was simply a distraction, to draw attention away. The cook put it there for us to follow a false lead. Kahn's obvious interest in corgis meant he'd be an ideal suspect. It was an accident that he slipped on it."

Lyv looked insulted at the idea. She did not like being fooled.

lead a clue or piece of evidence that could be true or useful | **suspect** sb you think committed a crime | **to look insulted** to show that you aren't happy about sth that sb said or did

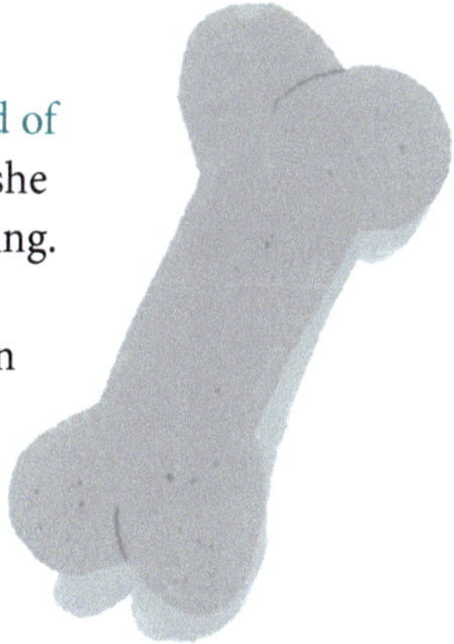

"Madame Soufflée also wanted to get rid of Sexton. His room was next to hers and she was afraid that he would notice something. That's why she wanted us to look at the butler. She must have known that Sexton was doing something illegal," Lyv concluded.

"So, all we had to do was to hide in the Corgi Room and wait for the kidnapper to return the dog. After all, Madame Soufflée didn't plan to hurt Skiddi once she had the diamond." Arthur finished.

"Amazing," the chief whistled. "I sent you to find the Queen's dog and you solved five additional crimes, including the theft of a famous diamond." He looked very impressed with his team.

"Indeed, sir," Young confirmed. "It was the sensible thing to do since I happened to be at the palace for the kidnapping case anyway."

to get rid of to throw sth away

Higgs and Lyv rolled their eyes.

At that moment an urgent knock on the door made everybody look up. Speed rushed into the office.

“Sir, there’s been a break-in at the Tower of London,” he panted.

“The Crown Jewels are missing. The Queen has sent for Inspector Young and his team …”

THE END

A Sum it up...

The three most important things that happened were:

1.

2.

3.

Think about it...

Why did MacAnguish get a promotion? Do you think he deserved it?

Can you list the five crimes that got solved by the police?

Activities

Focus on the story

1. Are these statements True or False?

Tick the correct box.

	True	False
1. Higgs Duncan was the youngest Scotland Yard detective ever.	☐	☐
2. Higgs likes wearing very colourful clothes.	☐	☐
3. Sexton was the Queen's gardener.	☐	☐
4. MacAnguish was the only person with the key to the garden door.	☐	☐
5. The dog's diet consists mainly of dog food and scraps.	☐	☐
6. The plants MacAnguish was cultivating were illegal.	☐	☐
7. Lyv was more comfortable doing physical tasks than interrogating suspects.	☐	☐
8. Prince Khan was upset when he was interrogated.	☐	☐
9. Prince Khan wanted to buy one of the Queen's corgis.	☐	☐
10. Jill wanted to breed corgis	☐	☐
11. The police arrested Jill because breeding corgis is illegal.	☐	☐
12. Arthur Young was clumsy.	☐	☐

2. What happened when?

Put the events in the correct order. Put the correct letter next to the number.

a.	Sexton told the police there had been a trespasser.	1 ......
b.	The Prince was found motionless on the floor.	2 ......
c.	Sexton was pardoned by the Queen.	3 ......
d.	Jill Banister was arrested.	4 ......
e.	Arthur followed MacAnguish all the way to Scotland.	5 ......
f.	Sexton was spotted in a betting house.	6 ......
g.	MacAnguish admitted he was growing thistles in the palace.	7 ......
h.	The blood found was confirmed to be human.	8 ......
i.	The investigators arrived at the Palace to investigate a crime.	9 ......
j	Madame Soufflée was attacked by a mysterious man.	10 ......

3. Where were they?

Put the following places in the order they were mentioned in the book.

...... a petrol station

...... the West End Central Police Station

...... Buckingham Palace

...... a betting office

...... Dunbar

...... the guest room at Buckingham Palace

...... Colony of Menampur

...... a dog daycare centre

4. What happened where?

Match the place with the event that happened there.

Where?	What?
1. Dunbar	a. The corgi was kidnapped here.
2. the guest room	b. Arthur bought doughnuts and coffee here.
3. the petrol station	c. Jill Banister was arrested here.
4. the dog daycare centre	d. The Prince was found unconscious here.
5. Buckingham Palace	e. MacAnguish had a croft here.

Focus on the people

1. Who did what?

Read the sentence and decide who did or said what.

a

b

c

d

e

Who …

1. … was given a promotion by the Queen.
2. … ate doughnuts and coffee at the petrol station.
3. … fed the dogs venison, wild goose and salmon.
4. … wanted to breed corgis.
5. … went to a betting house.
6. … was attacked in the street.
7. … cultivated endangered plants.
8. … left dogs at the dog daycare centre.
9. … was told off by the Queen.
10. … took lots of notes.

2. What are they like?

Complete the profiles for each of the characters. You can use your imagination!

 Higgs	 Arthur	 Lyv
Favourite food:	**Favourite food:**	**Favourite food:**
Things he doesn't like:	**Things he doesn't like:**	**Things she doesn't like:**
Strange possession:	**Strange possession:**	**Strange possession:**
Thing he wants:	**Thing he wants:**	**Thing she wants:**

Focus on grammar

1. Which word fits best?

Choose the right word to connect the sentences.

and	but	because	although	so

1. .... Arthur was aware that Lyv could do karate, he had never seen her in action.
2. Madame Soufflée fed the corgis venison .... she loves dogs.
3. Arthur Young doesn't mind working long hours .... he loves his job.
4. They didn't know who had committed the crime, ... they had a meeting to check all the evidence.
5. The Queen's corgi was missing .... nobody had demanded a ransom yet.

2. Gerund or infinitive?

Choose the correct option to complete the sentence.

1. Arthur fancied eating / to eat a doughnut.
2. The Prince offered buying / to buy one of the corgis
3. Arthur decided following / to follow Jill to see if she kidnapped the corgi.
4. Arthur considered calling / to call for backup when he was following Jill.
5. Sexton learnt fighting / to fight in his previous job.

Build your vocabulary

Focus on words and phrases

1. What's the word?

Unscramble the words so that they make up a word about crime and punishment.

1. vceindee		things that can make you think that something is true
2. icvtedtee		a person whose job it is to investigate a crime
3. trrsae		when the police take somebody into custody to ask them questions about a crime that they may have committed
4. roansm		money that is asked for in exchange for releasing somebody who has been kidnapped
5. inirettgoaorn		a series of questions asked to get information
6. puestsc		a person who is believed to have committed a crime

2. What do these phrasal verbs mean?

Match the phrasal verb with down to the definition.

1. to slow down	a. to make yourself fall on a surface
2. to pin someone down	b. to disappoint
3. to chase something down	c. to start moving more slowly
4. to flop down	d. to write down
5. to note down	e. to hold somebody on the floor
6. to let down	f. to follow and catch something

3. Where does the phrasal verb go?

Fill in the gap with the correct phrasal verb and write an example of your own by finishing the sentence or writing the next sentence.

a. She grabbed his wrists and .... him .... against the cold, hard floor ....

b. The inspector started to run. After a few steps he had to

....

c. She was tired so she .... on the sofa and waited.

....

d. The queen was .... by Sexton so she gave him a dressing-down. ....

e. She much preferred *action* .... leads ....

....

f. Arthur .... what the dogs ate for breakfast.

....

Arthur Young and the Corgi Mystery – the mind map

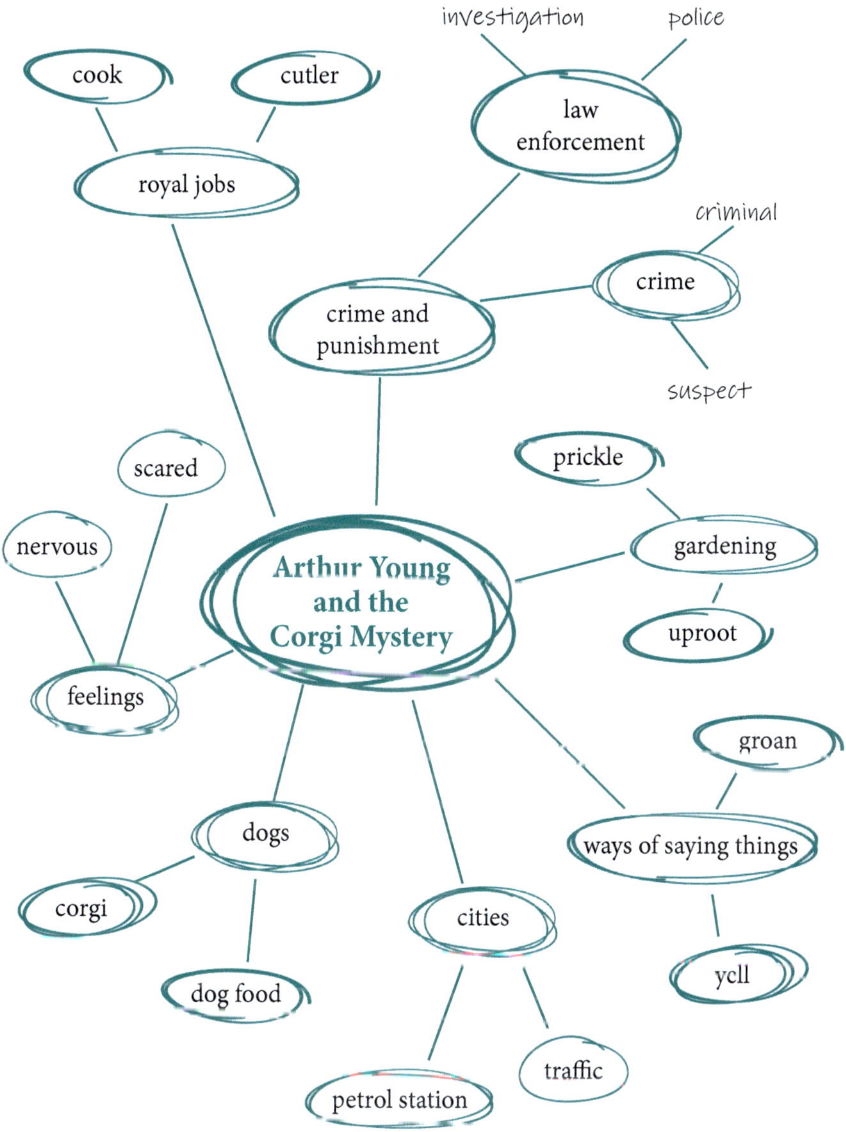

Glossary

	New word?	Notes / connected words
Food and drink		
cook	☐	
dog food	☐	
fresh vegetables	☐	
menu	☐	
salmon	☐	
venison	☐	
wild goose	☐	
Crime and punishment		
accomplice	☐	
armed	☐	
constable	☐	
cop	☐	
crime scene	☐	
detective	☐	
evidence	☐	
forensics	☐	
innocent	☐	
interrogate	☐	
investigator	☐	
kidnap	☐	
ransom	☐	
robber	☐	
solve a case	☐	
suspect	☐	
suspicious	☐	
trespasser	☐	
Royal jobs		
cook	☐	
butler	☐	
groomer	☐	

	New word?	Notes / connected words
Gardening		
conservatory	☐	
croft	☐	
cultivate	☐	
garden	☐	
prickle	☐	a cactus has lots of prickles
Cities		
buildings	☐	
cars	☐	
flea market	☐	
market	☐	
nail salon	☐	
parking space	☐	
pet store	☐	
petrol station	☐	
street	☐	
traffic	☐	
Ways of saying different things		
groan	☐	
grunt	☐	
say	☐	
scream	☐	
tell	☐	
yell	☐	
Feelings		
nervous	☐	
sad	☐	

Find out more

Queen Elizabeth II was very fond of corgis. Find 10 interesting facts about the Royal corgis. If you're reading this in class, then compare your findings with your partner.

Example: *Corgi means "dwarf dog".*

1.
2.
3.
4.
5.
6.
7.

8.
9.
10.

Lost dog poster

With your partner, create a poster to find a lost dog, and answer the following questions:

1. What type of dog is it?
2. Where was it last seen?
3. What reward are you going to give to the person who finds the dog?
4. How can they contact you?

Reading strategies

Learn to love reading

Reading is a key part of learning a language – it's also a key part of life! You can dive into other worlds, emotions, situations and learn about the world beyond your own.

Reading in your own language can be difficult, so you may find reading in another language even more of a challenge. The good news is that there are lots of things you can do to make reading less like hard work and more like fun!

Here are some ideas that can help you enjoy working with this Team Reader. You can read it on your own or as a team, but the important thing is that you understand what happens in the story.

What you can do if you are having trouble understanding the story

- **Reconstruct the text** – or at least the main ideas behind it. That's why we've introduced the Sum it up / Think about it boxes at the end of each chapter. You have an opportunity to decide what the three main events in the chapter are and then think about or discuss some questions about it. It could be helpful to write a short summary in your own words of what happened before moving on to the next chapter.

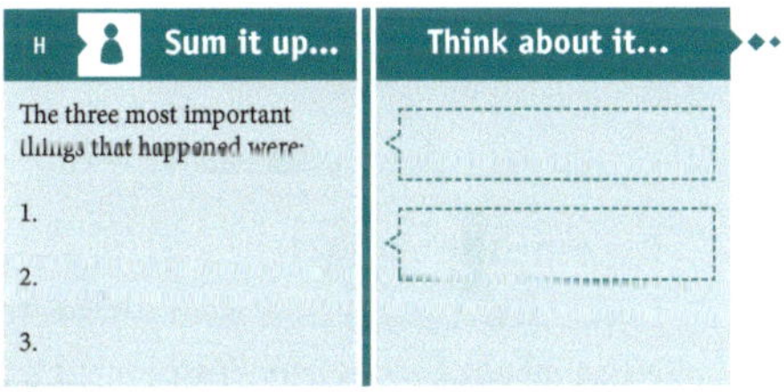

- **Use the pictures**
  Look at the illustrations. Describe what you can see and what you can remember about what you read. You could even look at the

illustrations before you read, guess what the story could be about, and then read to see if you are right.

- **Visualise what you have read**
  There are lots of ways of doing this. You can start by making a note of the key events, put them into order and then design a time line, a map, your own doodles – anything that helps you create your own visualisation of what happens in the story.

What you can do if you find the vocabulary too difficult

- **Make a note of key words**
  You can use the key words to connect your ideas and thoughts about what happened. If you want to make sentences and talk or write about what you have read the keywords will help.
- **Focus on what you can do**
  Even in your own language there will find words in texts that you don't know. If you're reading in another language this is sure to happen. Remember that this is normal and just continue to read. Try to work it out from the context. If you don't understand the sentence because the word is so important, then look it up or ask for help.

What you can do if you want to learn about a character

- **Become the character**
  Read all the parts that your character appears in. Note down key words. You could use the character profile box in the Activities section and add more information. Then try to tell the story as though you are the character. Don't worry about sticking to the facts, use your imagination to create the details that aren't in the text! Bring the character to life. What can you see? Smell? Hear? Feel? Taste?

What you can do if you want to learn about all the characters

- **Create a chart or table and add key facts**
  It's best if you design your own table, because then you can choose what you want to include. As an example though, you could use something simple like this. Simply note down key words that will help you remember what happened and why these words are relevant to the character.

Chapter	Lyv 	Arthur 	Higgs 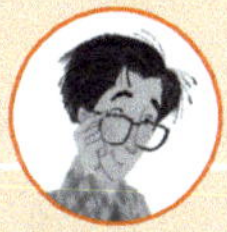
1			
2			
3			
4			
5			
6			
7			
8			
9			
10			
11			
12			
13			
14			
15			
16			
17			

Answer key

Focus on the story

1. 1. F, 2. T, 3. F, 4. T, 5. F, 6. F, 7. T, 8. T, 9. T, 10. T, 11. F, 12. T
2. i, a, e, f, b, g, h, j, d, c
3. 5, 7, 1, 4, 2, 6, 3, 8
4. 1. e, 2. d, 3. B, 4. C, 5. a

Focus on the people

1. 1. a, 2. c, 3. b, 4. e, 5. d, 6. B, 7. a, 8. e, 9. d, 10. c
2. Own answers.

Focus on grammar

1. 1. although, 2. and, 3. because, 4. so, 5. but
2. 1. eating, 2. to buy, 3. to follow, 4. calling, 5. to fight

Build your vocabulary

1. 1. evidence, 2. detective, 3. arrest, 4. ransom, 5. interrogation, 6. suspect
2. 1. c, 2, e, 3. f, 4. a, 5. d, 6. b
3. 1. pin him down, 2. slow down, 3. flop down, 4. let down, 5. chase leads up, 6. noted down

Who kidnapped Skiddi?

As he solves the case, Arthur takes a lot of notes. What do you think he wrote?

As you read the story, make a note of clues, strange behaviour and who you think did it.

Suspect 1

The suspect Name:

Job:

Anything else:

Their alibi

Reason for doing it

Strange behaviour

Clues and evidence

What I need to find out

Suspect 2

The suspect Name:
Job:
Anything else:

Their alibi

Reason for doing it

Strange behaviour

Clues and evidence

What I need to find out

Suspect 3

The suspect Name:

Job:

Anything else:

Their alibi

Reason for doing it

Strange behaviour

Clues and evidence

What I need to find out

Suspect 4

The suspect Name:

Job:

Anything else:

Their alibi

Reason for doing it

Strange behaviour

Clues and evidence

What I need to find out

Level 1	Pre-A1	200 words
Level 2	Pre-A1	400 words
Level 3	A1	600 words
Level 4	A1 +	800 words
Level 5	A2	1000 words
Level 6	A2 +	1250 words
Level 7	B1	1500 words
Level 8	B1 +	1750 words
Level 9	B2	2500 words

Now do the quizzes!

Photos:
9 Shutterstock (petite lili), New York; **122.1** Shutterstock (Richie Chan), New York; **122.2** Shutterstock (3DMI), New York; **133.1** Shutterstock (Atlas Agency), New York; **133.2** Shutterstock (Happy monkey), New York; **133.3** Shutterstock (Dora Zett), New York; **133.4** Shutterstock (Dreamzdesigners), New York; **133.5** Shutterstock (VectorPixelStar), New York; **134** Shutterstock (PEAPIZA), New York; **135** Shutterstock (Incomible), New York; **136** Shutterstock (IDCreativex), New York

1st edition 1 7 6 5 4 3 | 2029 28 27 26 25

DELTA Publishing, 2021
www.deltapublishing.co.uk

Authors Text: Don Haupt
Annotations and activities: Bernardo Morales
Editor: Kate Baade
Cover and layout: Andreas Drabarek / Eva Lettenmayer, Stuttgart, Germany
Illustrations: Gustavo Mazali
Design: Joachim Schrimm, ETYPO, Friolzheim, Germany
Cover picture: Gustavo Mazali
Druck und Bindung: Elanders Waiblingen GmbH

Printed in Germany
ISBN 978-3-12-530911-1